# HOPSCOTCH ADVENTURES

# The Sword in the Stone

Tales of King

First published in 2006 by
Franklin Watts
338 Euston Road
London
NW1 3BH

Franklin Watts Australia
Hachette Children's Books
Level 17/207 Kent Street
Sydney
NSW 2000

A CIP catalogue record for this book is available
from the British Library.

ISBN (10) 0 7496 6681 1(hbk)
ISBN (13) 978-0-7496-6681-1 (hbk)
ISBN (10) 0 7496 6694 3 (pbk)
ISBN (13) 978-0-7496-6694-1 (pbk)

**Series Editor:** Jackie Hamley
**Series Advisor:** Dr Barrie Wade
**Series Designer:** Peter Scoulding

Printed in China

Franklin Watts is a division of
Hachette Children's Books.

# The Sword in the Stone

by Karen Wallace and Neil Chapman

FRANKLIN WATTS
LONDON • SYDNEY

Once there was a time when war raged everywhere in Britain.

Britain did not have a king,
and the people were unhappy.

Merlin the magician knew that a strong king could stop the fighting.

So, Merlin put a special
sword in a block of stone.

Whoever
can pull this sword
from this stone
is the true
King of Britain

"There will be a tournament to find a king," he cried. "Every knight must try to pull out this sword."

9

In those days, a boy called Arthur
was a squire to a knight called
Sir Kay. Arthur looked after Sir
Kay's horse and armour.

Sir Kay with his father, Sir Ector, and
Arthur set off to the tournament.
Arthur was very excited.

When they arrived, Sir Kay realised
he had left his sword at an inn.
"Go back and get it," he told Arthur.

When Arthur got there, the inn was shut. He didn't know what to do. Suddenly he saw a sword in a block of stone in a churchyard.

14

Arthur quickly pulled it out
and ran back to Sir Kay.

Arthur gave the sword to Sir Kay,
who recognised it immediately.

"I have the sword, so I am the
king," Sir Kay said to his father.
But Sir Ector didn't believe him.

Then Arthur explained what he had done. "I must see for myself," said Sir Ector.

They went to the churchyard,
and Arthur put the sword back
in the stone.

Neither Sir Kay nor
Sir Ector could pull
it out again.

"It's easy," said Arthur.

He quickly drew out the sword.

Whoever
can pull this sword
from this stone
is the true
King of Britain

Sir Ector and Sir Kay fell to their
knees. "What are you doing?"
asked Arthur. "Read the words on
the stone," replied Sir Ector.

"You are the true king of Britain.

It has happened as Merlin said."

Arthur was amazed.

"Who is Merlin?" he cried.

23

Then Merlin appeared. "Arthur," he said, "your father was Uther, King of Britain. When you were a baby, I gave you to Sir Ector to keep you safe from jealous knights."

Arthur stared at the sword
and understood his duty.
"I promise to be a good king,"
he said.

At first the jealous knights would not accept him.

Again and again, they tried to pull the sword from the stone.

But only Arthur could do it.
At last the knights believed
what Merlin had told them.

"Long Live King Arthur!"
they cried.

Soon Arthur was crowned King. And for the first time since the death of Arthur's father, everyone in the land was happy.

31

Hopscotch has been specially designed to fit the requirements of the National Literacy Strategy. It offers real books by top authors and illustrators for children developing their reading skills.
There are 37 Hopscotch stories to choose from:

**Marvin, the Blue Pig**
ISBN 0 7496 4619 5

**Plip and Plop**
ISBN 0 7496 4620 9

**The Queen's Dragon**
ISBN 0 7496 4618 7

**Flora McQuack**
ISBN 0 7496 4621 7

**Willie the Whale**
ISBN 0 7496 4623 3

**Naughty Nancy**
ISBN 0 7496 4622 5

**Run!**
ISBN 0 7496 4705 1

**The Playground Snake**
ISBN 0 7496 4706 X

**"Sausages!"**
ISBN 0 7496 4707 8

**The Truth about Hansel and Gretel**
ISBN 0 7496 4708 6

**Pippin's Big Jump**
ISBN 0 7496 4710 8

**Whose Birthday Is It?**
ISBN 0 7496 4709 4

**The Princess and the Frog**
ISBN 0 7496 5129 6

**Flynn Flies High**
ISBN 0 7496 5130 X

**Clever Cat**
ISBN 0 7496 5131 8

**Moo!**
ISBN 0 7496 5332 9

**Izzie's Idea**
ISBN 0 7496 5334 5

**Roly-poly Rice Ball**
ISBN 0 7496 5333 7

**I Can't Stand It!**
ISBN 0 7496 5765 0

**Cockerel's Big Egg**
ISBN 0 7496 5767 7

**How to Teach a Dragon Manners**
ISBN 0 7496 5873 8

**The Truth about those Billy Goats**
ISBN 0 7496 5766 9

**Marlowe's Mum and the Tree House**
ISBN 0 7496 5874 6

**Bear in Town**
ISBN 0 7496 5875 4

**The Best Den Ever**
ISBN 0 7496 5876 2

**ADVENTURE STORIES**

**Aladdin and the Lamp**
ISBN 0 7496 6678 1 *
ISBN 0 7496 6692 7

**Blackbeard the Pirate**
ISBN 0 7496 6676 5 *
ISBN 0 7496 6690 0

**George and the Dragon**
ISBN 0 7496 6677 3 *
ISBN 0 7496 6691 9

**Jack the Giant-Killer**
ISBN 0 7496 6680 3 *
ISBN 0 7496 6693 5

**TALES OF KING ARTHUR**

**1. The Sword in the Stone**
ISBN 0 7496 6681 1 *
ISBN 0 7496 6694 3

**2. Arthur the King**
ISBN 0 7496 6683 8 *
ISBN 0 7496 6695 1

**3. The Round Table**
ISBN 0 7496 6684 6 *
ISBN 0 7496 6697 8

**4. Sir Lancelot and the Ice Castle**
ISBN 0 7496 6685 4 *
ISBN 0 7496 6698 6

**TALES OF ROBIN HOOD**

**Robin and the Knight**
ISBN 0 7496 6686 2 *
ISBN 0 7496 6699 4

**Robin and the Monk**
ISBN 0 7496 6687 0 *
ISBN 0 7496 6700 1

**Robin and the Friar**
ISBN 0 7496 6688 9 *
ISBN 0 7496 6702 8

**Robin and the Silver Arrow**
ISBN 0 7496 6689 7 *
ISBN 0 7496 6703 6

**\* hardback**